The Great
Seed Mystery
For Kids

The Great Seed Mystery For Kids

WRITER
PEGGY HENRY

PHOTOGRAPHERS
ALAN COPELAND AND BARRY SHAPIRO

ILLUSTRATOR
JAMES BALKOVEK

AVON BOOKS  NEW YORK

Product Manager: CYNTHIA FOLLAND, NK LAWN AND GARDEN CO.

Acquisition, Development and Production Services: BMR, Corte Madera, CA

Acquisition: JACK JENNINGS, BOB DOLEZAL

Series Concept: BOB DOLEZAL

Project Director: JANE RYAN

Developmental Editor: CYNTHIA PUTNAM

Horticulturist: BARBARA STREMPLE

Photographic Director: ALAN COPELAND

Cover Design: KAREN EMERSON

Art Director (cover): KARRYLL NASON

Art Director (interior): BRAD GREENE

Interior Art: JAMES BALKOVEK

Educational Review: ETHEL TEDSEN

Copy Editor: JANET VOLKMAN

Typography and Page Layout: BARBARA GELFAND

Models: ANNIE HENRY, VALERIE HENRY, MAX SHAPIRO

Color Separations: PREPRESS ASSEMBLY INCORPORATED

Printing and Binding: PENDELL PRINTING INC.

Production Management: THOMAS E. DORSANEO, JANE RYAN

First Avon Books Trade Printing: February 1993

Library of Congress Cataloging-in-Publication Data:
Henry, Peggy
    The great seed mystery / writer, Peggy Henry; photographers, Alan Copeland and Barry Shapiro, illustrator, James Balkovek.
        p. cm. – (NK Lawn & Garden step-by-step visual guide)
    Includes index.
    Summary: Projects and experiments demonstrate the significance of seeds, how and why they grow, and how to plant and care for a garden.
    ISBN: 0-380-76805-4
    1. Plant propagation—Juvenile literature. 2. Seeds—Juvenile literature. 3. Gardening—Juvenile literature. [1. Seeds—Experiments. 2. Plants—Experiments. 3. Gardening. 4. Experiments. 5. Science projects.]
    I. Copeland, Alan, ill. II. Shapiro, Barry, ill. III. Balkovek, James, ill. IV. Title. V. Series.
SB121.H46 1993
635'.0431–dc20
                                                          92-20193
                                                          CIP

Special thanks to: Tom Henry; Sonoma Mission Gardens Nursery, Sonoma, CA. Additional photo credits: Saxon Holt: pgs. 17, 18, 20-21, 24-25, 68-69.

Notice: The information contained in this book is true and complete to the best of our knowledge. All recommendations are made without any guarantees on the part of the authors, NK Lawn and Garden Co., or BMR. Because the means, materials and procedures followed by homeowners are beyond our control, the author and publisher disclaim all liability in connection with the use of this information.

AVON BOOKS
A division of
The Hearst Corporation
1350 Avenue of the Americas
New York, New York 10019

AVON TRADEMARK REG. U.S. PAT. OFF.
AND IN OTHER COUNTRIES, MARCA
REGISTRADA, HECHO EN U.S.A.

92   93   94   95   96   10   9   8   7   6   5   4   3   2   1

TABLE OF CONTENTS

Exploring the World of Seeds......................6–7
A Seed Hunt...8–9
How Flowers Make Seeds.........................10–11
Inside a Flower....................................12–13
Getting Seeds to Sprout..........................14–15
Light, Water, Air and Food.......................16–17
Big Seeds..18–19
Seed Sprouting Times.............................20–21
A Plant Food Factory.............................22–23
Plant Parts..24–25
Trees..26–27
A Sunflower Secret................................28–29
Growing Your Own Garden........................30–31
Starting Seeds Indoors............................32–33
Planting Outdoors.................................34–35
Gardening Hints...................................36–37
Easy Flowers to Grow.............................38–39
Using Tools Properly..............................40–41
How to Pollinate Flowers.........................42–43
Collecting Seeds...................................44–45
How Seeds Travel..................................46–47
Disappearing Seeds................................48–49
Cycles in Nature...................................50–51
Seeds that Grow Underground.....................52–53
Growing Alfalfa Sprouts...........................54–55
Measuring Seed Production........................56–57
Testing Seed Strength.............................58–59
Seed Survival......................................60–61
Sensitive Plants...................................62–63
Dried Flowers.....................................64–65
Pressed Flowers...................................66–67
A Bean Magic Trick...............................68–69
Dried Gourds......................................70–71
Tasty Seeds..72–73
Wildflowers.......................................74–75
World Without Seeds..............................76–77
Index..78–79

EXPLORING THE WORLD OF SEEDS

Look at all the products on this page. Are they things you like to eat or drink? You probably have some of them around your house. Do you know where they come from? How many of them do you think come from seeds?

Ground coffee beans

Cup of coffee

Cocoa powder

Flour

Mug of hot chocolate

Poppy seeds on bagel

Bread

Peppercorns

Peanut butter

Jam

A SEED ADVENTURE

Seeds are everywhere. They're inside fruits, vegetables, flowers, trees and even weeds. Seeds are an important part of the natural world all around you.

A lot of what you eat comes from seeds. The peanuts in peanut butter are seeds. The cocoa beans that give us chocolate are seeds. The flour in bread and cookies is made from seeds.

Have you ever wondered what a seed is and where it comes from or what makes it grow? We're going to try to solve these mysteries. Come along as we explore the world of seeds and look for clues. You'll try lots of fun projects and experiments. You'll even grow seeds in your own garden.

First you'll find out what seeds are. You'll experiment with getting them to sprout, and you'll discover how they grow.

You'll see how flowers, plants and trees fit into the puzzle. You'll collect seeds and find out how they survive in nature. You'll even solve the mystery of sleeping seeds.

You'll see how seeds get free rides to lots of places. And you'll even crack the case of the disappearing seeds. You'll also search underground for some very unusual seeds.

You'll make things, you'll watch things, and you'll wonder. But one thing is for sure—you'll have loads of fun. So let's not wait. The adventure is about to begin.

A Seed Hunt

Let's do some detective work. Some seeds are easy to recognize, like apple seeds; others are not as obvious, like peas in a pod or nuts in a shell. Some seeds, like coconuts, may not look like seeds at all. How many different seeds can you find in your house or garden?

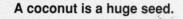
A coconut is a huge seed.

An apple has dark seeds in its core.

Pine cones have seeds on their scales.

Tomatoes have lots of seeds inside.

A banana has many seeds inside.

Kernels of corn are seeds.

A strawberry has many tiny seeds on the outside.

Inside a peanut you'll find two large seeds.

WHAT ARE SEEDS?

Seeds are amazing little packages of life. Hidden inside a seed is a tiny plant just waiting to grow. It has two very small leaves, a stem and the beginnings of the first root. The seed also has enough food around the little plant to feed it until the plant is big enough to make its own food. Are seeds alive? Yes!

All flowering plants, including trees and vegetables, grow from seeds. We know that seeds give us good things to eat. They also grow into plants and trees, which give off the oxygen we need to breathe.

Part of what makes a seed so special is the secret code that it has inside. The code tells a seed just how to grow. A seed knows which direction to send roots and which direction to send leaves—even if you plant it upside-down. It knows what kind of plant to become, how big to get and what kind of flowers or fruit to make.

Open a package of mixed flower seeds and look at the seeds with a magnifying glass. What do you see? The seeds are all very different, just as the plants that they become will all be different, too.

Some seeds are as small as a ladybug's footprint. One special seed, a coconut, weighs as much as a bowling ball! Seeds come in all shapes and colors, too. On your seed hunt you'll have to be on the lookout for all sorts of seeds.

How Flowers Make Seeds

A seed's life is part of a cycle. First a seed sprouts and grows into a plant. Soon flowers appear. Inside the flowers, new seeds begin to grow. Now we're back where we started.

First A seed is formed. Sometimes it grows inside a pod, like these sweet pea seeds. When the pod is ripe, it opens and the seeds are ready to fall to the ground and grow. Soon they sprout and become seedlings.

Next The flower begins to fade, and the petals start to fall off. You can see the tiny sweet pea pod forming. The little seeds are inside the pod as it grows.

Then The seedlings grow into plants. Soon the plants form buds that open into flowers. The plant will make many flowers over its lifetime.

Finally The pod splits open, and you can see the seeds inside. The life cycle of this sweet pea is complete, but it is just starting for the new seeds.

WHERE SEEDS COME FROM

Plants make flowers, and flowers produce seeds so new little plants can grow. This cycle, going around and around, has helped plants to survive for a very long time.

How exactly does a seed come from a flower? Let's see if we can trace what happens inside the flower.

It all starts with the female and the male parts of the flower. In the female part of the flower are the tiny seeds-to-be. In the male part of the flower is a yellow dust called *pollen*.

When the yellow dust travels to the tiny seeds-to-be in the female parts of the flower, the young seeds begin to form. This is called *pollination*.

Bees, bugs, butterflies and birds help with pollination. When they land inside the petals of a flower and move around, they brush pollen onto the female parts of the flower. This allows the young seeds to develop. Sometimes wind or droplets of water can scatter the pollen, too.

If a flower has no help with pollination, it usually can't make seeds. Pollen must get onto the female parts of the flower for seeds to form. We can thank wind, water, insects and birds for their parts in pollinating flowers.

INSIDE A FLOWER

Let's look closely at flower parts to see how seeds are made. Choose a big flower like this Iceland poppy so the male and female parts are easier to see. You'll use a magnifying glass to look for clues.

You can probably already identify the petals and the stem. In the center of the flower is a fat stalk. This is the *pistil*, or female part of the flower. Sometimes it is slender. Open the pistil. In pockets at the bottom are many tiny seeds-to-be, called *ovules*.

Around the pistil are taller, skinnier stalks with a fine yellow dust on the tips. These male parts of the flower are called *stamens*. At the tip of each stamen is a tiny case called an *anther*. When ready, the anthers open, showing fine yellow grains of pollen inside. If you touch the anther, does pollen get on your finger? Pollen must get to the top of the pistil and reach down to the ovules for seeds to form.

Now look at other flowers and see if you can find these parts. Try an apple blossom or a pansy or a lily. Do all the flowers have a pistil and stamens? Some kinds of plants may not have female parts and male parts on the same flower.

Pistil The pistil in the center of the flower contains the seeds.

Seeds Seeds, which contain new plants, will form at the bottom of the pistil.

Stamens The stamens surround the pistil. They have thin stalks called *filaments* that support the anthers.

Stem The stem attaches the flower to the plant.

Petals Petals make colorful, sometimes sweet-smelling rings around the pistil. They are the showy part of the flower.

Anther The tiny anther is a case filled with pollen.

13

GETTING
SEEDS TO SPROUT

What Do Seeds Need?

Seeds need certain things to sprout. Can you guess what? Water? Soil? Light? Air? Let's experiment with lima bean seeds and find out what they need. Besides seeds, you'll need five jars, soil and cotton.

Fill the first jar with water and drop in a seed. Will water alone be enough to sprout the seed?

Put dry soil in the second jar and set a seed on top. Do not water the seed. See if a seed can sprout without water.

Put moist soil in the third jar and again set a seed on top. Put this jar in a dark place. Will it sprout without light?

For the fourth jar, soak some cotton in water and lightly squeeze it out. Put the seed on top of the cotton. Will it sprout on this moist surface?

Fill the fifth jar with moist soil and put a seed on top. This time, put the jar near a sunny window. Keep the soil moist. Now have you given the seed all it needs to sprout?

Wait a week or more and see what happens. Without air the seed in jar one swells up, starts to sprout and dies. It suffocates. Without water, the seed in jar two cannot swell, open up and start growing. In the dark, and in the light on the cotton and on the moist soil, the seeds sprouted. They had moisture and air.

Look closely at the seedlings that have sprouted. They have two important things. They have water and air. Can you see the tiny root and the first leaves? It's a start!

LIGHT, WATER, AIR AND FOOD

This seedling, grown in moist soil in the dark, sprouted and grew very long looking for light. Besides water, air and soil, a seedling needs light to make its own food and grow.

This seedling, grown in moist cotton, lived for a few weeks on food stored in the seed. But it couldn't make it on water, air and light alone. A seedling needs nutrients from soil. They're like vitamins for a seedling and help it grow.

This seedling survived because it had water, light, air and soil. With these things, the seedling could make its own food and keep growing.

A SEED LUNCH BOX

In the experiment on pages 14–15, we got seeds to sprout. But what keeps a seedling alive?

Inside a seed are two main parts. One part is the tiny plant waiting to grow. The other part has food to keep the seedling alive after it sprouts.

Soak a bean seed in water overnight and carefully split it open. Do you see the beginnings of the tiny plant? It is the same color as the seed—you may need a magnifying glass to see it. The rest of the seed around the tiny plant holds the food. It's like a big lunch box for the seed!

The seedling needs this food to grow a stem and roots. Once the food from the seed is used up, that part dries up and drops off. Then the seedling must use its new roots to get nutrients and its new leaves to make its own food using energy from the sun.

In the picture below, the bean on the left has just sprouted and has food. The bean on the right used up its food from the seed. It is getting nutrients from the soil. Now the plant is on its own.

BIG SEEDS

Some plants with very large seeds can be grown in water. They can go a long time without soil because their seeds store so much food. Let's sprout a big seed—an avocado—and watch it grow. Although it won't make avocados, it will grow into a small tree.

Sprouting Avocado Seeds

First Space three toothpicks evenly around the middle of the seed, with the seed's pointed end facing up. The toothpicks will balance the seed over the jar.

Third In a few weeks the seed will split open. A root will grow out of the bottom, and a stem will come up through the middle of the seed. Move the jar to a sunny window.

Second Set the avocado, flat side down, into a jar of water. The water should always cover the bottom third of the seed. Put the jar in a warm, shady place.

Last Soon the first two leaves will show. You can pot the seed now, but it can grow in the water for many months.

SEED SPROUTING TIMES

Now we come to the case of sleeping seeds. Our mission is to find out why seeds start to grow when they do. All the seedlings in this picture were planted on the same day. Yet they each sprouted at different times. Let's find out why.

TOMATO SPROUTED IN 7 DAYS

BEAN SPROUTED IN 5 DAYS

NASTURTIUM SPROUTED IN 6 DAYS

RADISH SPROUTED IN 4 DAYS

PUMPKIN SPROUTED IN 6 DAYS

SLEEPING SEEDS

Seeds seem to have built-in time clocks. Some grow right away. Others wait for months or even years. The seeds in the picture were planted on the same day. The pots tell how long it took for each seed to sprout. Can you guess why seeds sprout at different times?

Seeds sprout when conditions for their survival are right. Sprouting time may depend on the time of year or temperature or light. It may depend on how thick the seed coat, or covering, is. It may even depend on the chemicals inside a seed that tell the seed when to grow.

Seeds that don't last long start growing right away. Seeds with thin coverings are like this. They must sprout quickly before they dry up.

Many seeds are formed in the autumn but don't start growing until the spring. Can you guess why? It's because the seedling would not live through the cold winter.

What would happen if all seeds sprouted at the same time? They might not all have enough room or water. They might all be lost in a freeze or a drought.

Over millions of years, seeds have developed patterns that help them survive. Sometimes they wait to sprout until the weather is right. Sometimes they wait for enough light or water. This gives them the best chance to grow into mature plants.

A Plant Food Factory

Fruit

Flower

Leaves

Stem

Roots

PLANTS MAKE THEIR OWN FOOD

Once a seedling becomes a plant, it makes its own food. The roots and stems send water and nutrients to the leaves. The leaves use water, nutrients, light, air and a mysterious ingredient called *chlorophyll* to make the food. The little plant is like a magician changing one thing into another. Let's see what each plant part does in the magic act.

Roots get water and nutrients from the soil. Roots also anchor the plant in the ground and store food that the leaves make.

Stems have tiny tubes that carry water and nutrients from the roots to the leaves. The tubes also carry the food made by the leaves back down to the roots. Stems hold up the plant.

Leaves make the food for the plant. They use nutrients from the soil, light from the sun, air and water. Chlorophyll, the part of a leaf that makes it green, helps the leaves turn these ingredients into food.

Flowers are important because they make more seeds. This keeps the cycle going for all kinds of plants from weeds to trees.

Fruits are coverings that protect seeds. Some fruits cover just one seed, as with a peach. Sometimes fruits cover many seeds, like tomatoes and apples. Sometimes many tiny seeds cover the fruit, as with a strawberry.

Plants are very special because they make their own food. Even though plants make their own food, people and animals cannot. They depend on plants for food. Without plants, people and animals could not survive.

PLANT PARTS

Look at the vegetables on this page. Can you tell what part of each plant is eaten? Sometimes we eat the roots or stems. Sometimes we like the leaves or flowers.

Peas

Beans

Celery

Broccoli

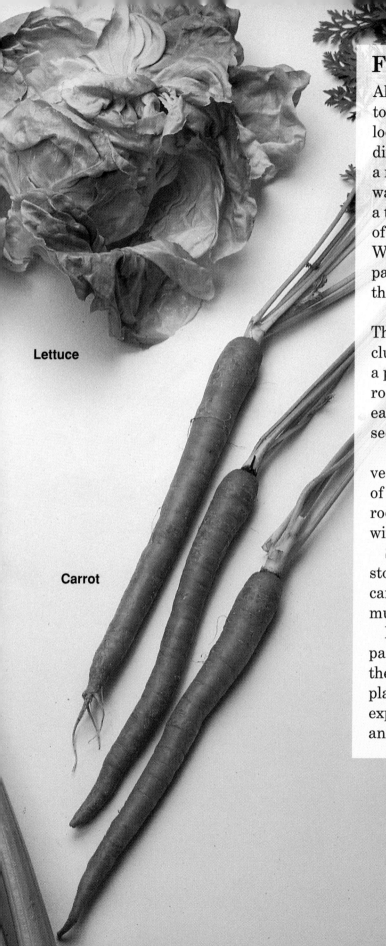

Lettuce

Carrot

Fruits and Vegetables

All plants need the same basic parts to grow. But those parts don't always look the same. A tree root looks different from a carrot, which is also a root. A tomato is nothing like a walnut, yet both are seed covers. And a tree trunk isn't anything like a stalk of celery—or is it? Both are stems. When you look closely, you see the parts may look different, but they do the same jobs.

Sometimes the parts are edible. The broccoli that you eat is really clusters of flower buds. When you eat a pea, you eat the seed. You eat the root of a carrot, and with lettuce you eat the leaves. With beans you eat the seed pod, seeds and all.

Often the part that is edible grows very big—bigger than on other kinds of plants. This is true with carrot roots and lettuce leaves. It's also true with large seeds like peas and beans.

Sometimes the parts help the plant store food, water and nutrients. A carrot root does this. And think how much moisture is in a juicy apple.

Don't let the plants fool you. Identify parts by what they do, not just how they look. And remember that not all plant parts are edible. Before you experiment with any plant, check with an adult helper first.

TREES

Trees have the same life cycle as most plants. They start from a seed and grow up to make flowers or cones with new seeds inside. Can you match each tree here to the seed it comes from? (Answers at bottom of page 27.)

Oak

Maple

Palm

A

B

C

Redwood

SEED SECRETS

Tree seeds, like all other seeds, contain information. That information tells the seed what kind of tree to become. It tells the tree when to start growing, how big to get and what kind of leaves or flowers to make.

Most trees make seeds from flowers, as other plants do. The seeds form inside the flowers. Some trees make seeds in cones. If pollen from the tree is blown by the wind and lands inside the cone, seeds form.

We know seeds come in all different sizes. But does a large seed always make a great big tree?

Look at the tallest tree in the world, the coast redwood of California. It makes little cones with seeds that are as small as the head of a pin. The coconut is the biggest seed in the world. Yet it grows into a palm tree much smaller than the redwood.

Sometimes seeds of different sizes grow into trees of the same size. An apple tree grows from a small seed and gets about as big as a peach tree, which comes from a big seed.

The trees in the picture all grow to different sizes. All of their seeds are very different. We can't tell by the size of the seed how big the tree will become. That's a secret that stays locked inside a seed until it grows. [**Answer**: (A)—maple seed; (B)—redwood cone and seed; (C)—coconut (palm tree); (D)—acorn (oak)]

D

A SUNFLOWER SECRET

A sunflower looks like one big flower, but it has a secret. It's really made of lots of little flowers, which you can find in the flower's center. There's a seed behind each little flower.

Petals The big petals around the outside of the sunflower are attached to flowers. These special flowers, each with one petal, are called *ray flowers*.

Flowers The little flowers in the center of this sunflower have no petals, but under each flower a seed will form.

ONE OR MANY?

Flowers come in many shapes and sizes. They make seeds in lots of different ways. The sunflower looks like one big flower, but it isn't. It's a collection of many small flowers called *florets*. Cosmos and daisies are like this, too.

You can see in the sunflower that each little floret forms only one seed. These flowers need many florets to produce enough seeds to keep the cycle going.

A geranium (shown below) has its florets in clusters. Many single florets on one stalk form a big flower. Each of these florets will form a seed.

Some flowers do not have florets. Their petals are part of one single flower. In the center many seeds are formed together, instead of in separate florets. Poppies are an example of a flower without florets.

GROWING YOUR OWN GARDEN

Sunflower

Tomato

Gomphrena

Dwarf Cosmos

Marigold

Sweet Alyssum

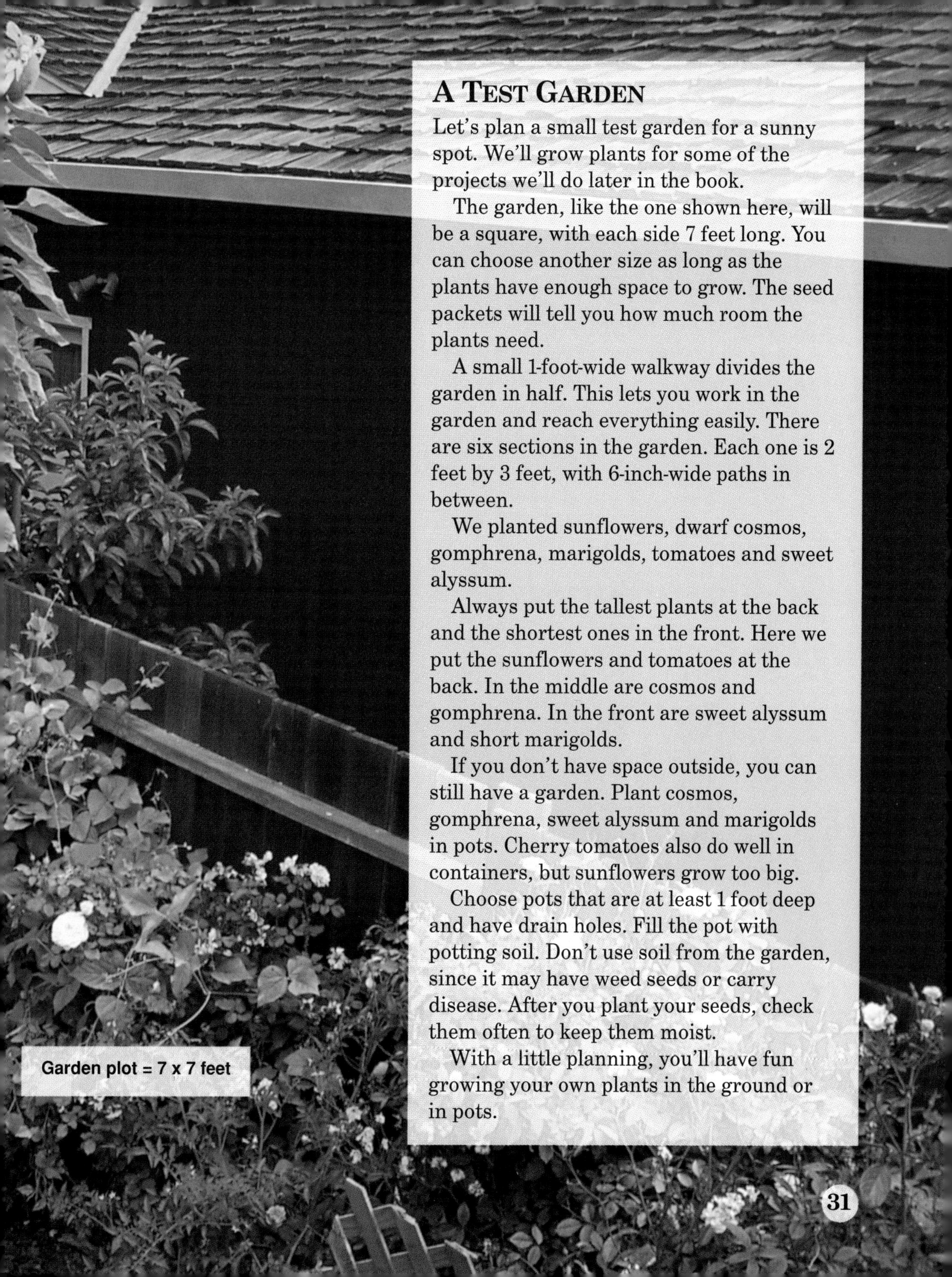

A TEST GARDEN

Let's plan a small test garden for a sunny spot. We'll grow plants for some of the projects we'll do later in the book.

The garden, like the one shown here, will be a square, with each side 7 feet long. You can choose another size as long as the plants have enough space to grow. The seed packets will tell you how much room the plants need.

A small 1-foot-wide walkway divides the garden in half. This lets you work in the garden and reach everything easily. There are six sections in the garden. Each one is 2 feet by 3 feet, with 6-inch-wide paths in between.

We planted sunflowers, dwarf cosmos, gomphrena, marigolds, tomatoes and sweet alyssum.

Always put the tallest plants at the back and the shortest ones in the front. Here we put the sunflowers and tomatoes at the back. In the middle are cosmos and gomphrena. In the front are sweet alyssum and short marigolds.

If you don't have space outside, you can still have a garden. Plant cosmos, gomphrena, sweet alyssum and marigolds in pots. Cherry tomatoes also do well in containers, but sunflowers grow too big.

Choose pots that are at least 1 foot deep and have drain holes. Fill the pot with potting soil. Don't use soil from the garden, since it may have weed seeds or carry disease. After you plant your seeds, check them often to keep them moist.

With a little planning, you'll have fun growing your own plants in the ground or in pots.

Garden plot = 7 x 7 feet

STARTING SEEDS INDOORS

Sometimes seeds grow better if they are started indoors. If it's too cold outside, seeds won't sprout or may be harmed by frost. By starting seeds indoors, you give them a head start. The plants will be at least six weeks old when they start life in the garden.

The seed packet will tell you when to plant your seeds indoors. Be careful. If you start seeds too early, they'll be too thin and tall or *leggy* by the time it's warm enough to plant them outside.

It's easy to start seeds inside. Here we're starting marigolds in an egg carton, but you can use a milk carton or other container. You can also buy starter kits at the store. Just be sure the little plants stay moist and get lots of light after they sprout.

Before you plant the seedlings outdoors, let them get used to the cooler temperatures and bright sunlight little by little. This is called *hardening off*. Begin by placing the seedlings outdoors in a spot protected from direct wind and frost. If it's really warm, keep them in partial shade. For the first few days, leave them for about an hour before bringing them back inside. After that, let them stay outside a little longer each day. In a couple of weeks, the plants will be ready to go into the garden.

Egg Carton Planter

First Use a pencil or pen to poke a hole in each cup of the egg carton. Poke from the inside out. This is for drainage.

Fourth Drop two marigold seeds in each cup. Cover with 1/4 inch of soil. For other seeds, read the seed packet.

Second Fill each cup with potting soil. Don't use soil from the garden. Place the carton in a tray or pan.

Fifth Label the tray and cover it with plastic wrap. Poke a few holes to let air in. Place tray in a sunny south-facing window. Remove the plastic when the seeds sprout.

Third Fill the tray with warm water. Wait several minutes for the soil to soak up the water. Pour the extra water into the sink.

Last If both seeds sprout, clip off the smaller one. When the weather is warm enough, harden off the seedlings and plant outdoors.

PLANTING OUTDOORS

GETTING READY TO PLANT

Preparing the garden will help your seeds or little plants get off to the right start. It will also help make the garden easier to take care of.

An important step is preparing the soil. With an adult helper, turn the soil over with a fork or hoe. This loosens the soil so the roots can grow easily. Be sure to remove any weeds you turn up.

Next you can mix in 3–4 inches of compost to loosen and enrich the soil. Compost is made of decaying animal and plant matter. It helps add nutrients to the soil.

Have an adult help you work in an all-purpose fertilizer, following the directions on the package. Finally, rake the area smooth.

You'll plant some seeds in rows, others in hills. Check the seed packet to see what each seed needs. The seed packet has all the tips you need for planting, such as when to plant in your area. An adult helper can help you understand the information on the seed packet.

Careful planning and preparing will help your garden grow into a fun and exciting place.

Plan the garden first, then lay out beds by using string to mark the rows where you will plant your seeds or seedlings. Next turn the soil over and mix in compost and fertilizer to improve the soil and to add nutrients.

To reach each part of the garden, you need paths. Keep them from becoming muddy by covering them with bark, straw or leaves.

Most seeds are planted in rows. Some, including many flower seeds, can be poked into the soil without digging. Plant carrots, peas, radishes or sunflowers in rows.

To transplant, use your fingers to gently loosen any tangled roots, leaving some of the soil around the roots. Set the seedling in the soil no higher or lower than it was in the container. Then gently firm the soil around the base of the plant and water.

PLANTING AND TRANSPLANTING

Use string to mark straight rows. Be sure the rows are far enough apart so the plants have room, and so you can weed and water. Use your finger to make a line along the top of the row. Tap the seeds out of the packet, spacing them as far apart as the package says. Cover the seeds and pat down the soil with your hands. Water gently.

For hills, pull the soil together with the hoe to make a mound about 12 inches wide and 6 inches high. Spread seeds evenly around the top of the mound and gently poke them down into the soil. Cover them and pat the soil all over the mound. Water carefully.

Certain plants grow better on hills than in rows. They spread out in all directions and need plenty of space. Cucumbers, birdhouse gourds and many kinds of squash do well on hills.

As your seedlings sprout you may have to remove some. This is called *thinning* them. If they're too close together, they won't grow well. The seed package tells you how far apart they should be.

To transplant a seedling, dig a hole big enough for the rootball. Carefully turn the container upside down and tap the plant out. Never pull it out by the stem, because you might break the stem or tear the roots. Set the seedling into the hole and fill soil in around it. Press gently but firmly around the bottom of the plant. Finish by making a ring of soil around the plant to catch water.

GARDENING HINTS

Use a gentle overhead spray to water young plants. Water mature plants at the bottom of the stem. Try not to wet the whole plant.

Leaves, compost or straw make good mulching materials. Keep mulch 2–3 inches away from the stem of the plant.

For plants close to the ground, fill the ring around the plant with water. This keeps leaves dry. Let the water soak into the soil and water again.

Pull weeds by hand when seedlings are small. Use a hoe carefully around larger plants. Cut weeds off at the roots, or uproot them completely.

Snails and slugs like to feed in the mornings and evenings. Be sure to check underneath leaves for snails, slugs and other pests.

Here we're sprinkling fertilizer around the plant and working it into the ground. Wear gloves. Always follow the package instructions.

Taking care of your garden means remembering to water, mulch, weed, feed and check for bugs.

Watering comes first—right after planting. Water seeds carefully. Use a watering can or hose sprayer that makes mist, so you don't wash the seeds away. When watering small plants, use a gentle stream near the bottom of the plants or a gentle spray from the hose. Check often to see if the soil feels dry or if the plants are wilting or drooping. If this happens, you need to water.

Mulch helps keep the soil moist and weeds out. Mulching means covering the soil around the plant with two to three inches of leaves, straw or compost.

Weeding is important because weeds steal water, sunlight and nutrients from plants. When your seedlings are small, weed by hand. Later you can use a hoe between rows, but have an adult helper nearby, since the hoe has a sharp edge.

Be on the lookout for bugs that may be eating your plants. Look for chewed leaves or flower petals, or shiny tracks from snails and slugs. Wearing your gloves, pick off any bugs, caterpillars, snails or slugs you see.

You'll also need an adult helper when you fertilize your plants. Some fertilizers are sprinkled on the dirt and mixed in. Some are mixed in water and poured onto the plant. Wear gloves when you handle fertilizers.

You'll soon see it's fun to take care of the garden and watch plants grow big.

EASY FLOWERS TO GROW

Growing your own flowers from seed is great fun. You can be creative and choose flowers of different sizes, shapes and colors to make a beautiful garden.

Find a spot for your flower bed and choose plants for either sun or shade, depending on what your bed gets. Plant short flowers in front, tall ones in back and in-between kinds in the center. Choose your favorite colors.

If you start seeds indoors, read the seed packets. Start the ones that take longest first. (See pages 32–33.)

Here we've chosen eight flowers that are easy to grow. Sweet alyssum is a fragrant, low plant good for the edge of the bed. Verbenas are a little taller, and so are marigolds and phlox. Next come zinnias and bachelor's buttons. Last are the tall cosmos.

You can plant special gardens for fragrance or for cut flowers. Sweet alyssum, stock, candytuft and nasturtium are fragrant. For cut flowers try bachelor's button, zinnia, aster, clarkia, coneflower, dahlia and gloriosa daisy.

Most flowers have a common and a scientific name. The scientific name has two parts and names plants exactly; a common name is like a nickname. It may vary from area to area.

Bachelor's Button
Centaurea cyanus

Marigold
Tagetes species

Phlox
Phlox drummondii

Cosmos
Cosmos species

Zinnia
Zinnia elegans

Verbena
Verbena hybrida

Sweet Alyssum
Lobularia maritima

39

Using Tools Properly

Potting Soil

Rake

Fork

Shovel

Stakes

Weeding Tool

Egg Carton

Trowel

String

Markers

Brush

TOOLS, EQUIPMENT AND HELP

To grow a garden, you need more than seeds and soil. You need the right tools and sometimes help from a friend.

Most of what you need you probably have around the house—like string and egg or milk cartons to grow seeds in.

Bigger tools are useful, too. A spading fork helps break up the soil and dig up plants without breaking their roots. A rake smooths the seedbed and gets big rocks out. Weeding, digging and forming rows is easy with a hoe.

A smaller hand digger and trowel help you dig between the plants and plant seedlings.

Wash all your tools after you use them and put them away in a safe place. They will last longer and you will always be able to find them.

Adult helpers are very important— especially when you are using tools with sharp edges. They'll show you how to use tools correctly and safely. They'll give you tips, such as always leaving the rake on the ground with the points down so you don't step on the points and get hurt.

Adult friends are great when you need to buy soil, seeds or pots. They'll help you carry the heavy stuff and work right beside you in the garden.

Sometimes adults help you read the seed packets so you can plan your garden. They'll help you get started and even remind you when it's time to water or care for the garden. Best of all, your helpers are friends to share your gardening fun with.

41

HOW TO POLLINATE FLOWERS

WHAT IS POLLINATION?

Let's see what really happens in pollination. It starts with pollen—the yellow dust that is made in the stamen, or male part of the flower. This pollen needs to reach the bottom of the female pistil for seeds to form.

The pollen is held in anthers—the little sacks on the tip of the stamen. In the center of the flower is the pistil. Inside the pistil, at the bottom, is an ovary where the seeds will form.

Insects, wind, birds and even water can brush or blow the pollen from the anther onto the top of the pistil. When the pollen finds its way down the pistil to the ovary, seeds start to grow.

Not all pollination happens the same way. Incomplete flowers are flowers that have either male or female parts but not both. Pollen from the male flower must get to the female flower for pollination to work. For complete flowers—those with both parts on the same flower—pollination is easier, since the pollen doesn't have far to travel.

Pollination is important because without it we would not have new seeds or plants. The answer to the mystery of pollination lies in the seeds!

With a small paintbrush (like the kind in a water-color set) brush the pollen off the anther of a yellow cosmos. You should be able to see the yellow dust on the tip of the brush.

Using the same brush, dust the pollen granules onto the pistil of the red cosmos. Put a tag on the flower to show it was the one pollinated. You'll collect the seeds later.

BE A PLANT SCIENTIST

We know pollination leads to seeds. (See pages 10–11.) Sometimes the seeds come from two parent plants. The new seedlings will have a combination of traits from each parent. In the same way, you may have brown hair from your mother or blue eyes from your father.

Scientists often pollinate plants that have different traits to develop new kinds of plants. The new plants may have different colors, grow bigger or make better fruits and vegetables than the parent plants.

Let's be plant scientists and pollinate the cosmos flowers in our test garden. Choose a yellow and a red cosmos. Brush the pollen from one onto the pistil of the other with a small paintbrush. You can experiment with another kind of flower, as long as the parents are the same kind of flower and different colors. Take a picture of the parent plants so you can compare them to the new plant when it grows.

Collect the seeds (see pages 44–45) after the flower fades and plant them. See if the flowers are the same colors as the parents.

The science of growing plants is full of surprises. New plants are created all the time. Someday you might be one of the scientists working on new and better plants.

COLLECTING SEEDS

This picture shows a pod from a cosmos flower that has formed seeds. The seeds are ready to be collected. If you gently pull the center of the dried flower, the seeds will come out. When you plant the seeds, the whole cycle—from seedling to flower to new seeds—will begin again.

Seed Head Wait for the flower to fade and the petals to fall so seeds can ripen.

Most seeds, like these poppy seeds, fall out easily. That makes it easy for the plant to keep the cycle going. Here, the seeds shake out of little holes in the top of the pistil.

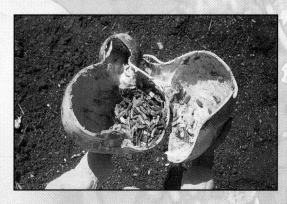

Sometimes you must open the pod yourself, as with this gourd. With an adult helper, cut open the pod to remove the seeds.

HARVEST TIME

Although seeds form at the end of the flower's life, they hold the beginnings of new life. They're like a bridge from the past into the future.

Collecting and planting seeds is a way to help build this bridge. First you must wait for the seeds to finish growing inside the flower. The flower will fade and the petals will fall. You'll know the seeds are ready when the pod dries and begins to open.

You can collect seeds from many flowers by shaking the flower upside down into a plastic bag. With some, like a cosmos or marigold, you can pull out the seeds all at once from the center of the flower. Make sure seeds are dry before storing them in a covered jar. Keep them in a cool place until you plant them.

Most seeds will sprout right away if the soil is warm enough. But some need to go through a cold spell first.

You'll probably find that most flowers make many, many seeds. Not all the seeds will have the right conditions to grow, so the plant produces many seeds to make sure some seeds will live and keep the cycle going.

Watch the cycle as the flowers bloom and make seeds. Have fun as you search for and collect seeds to keep your garden growing.

How Seeds Travel

A FREE RIDE

Seeds are clever little travelers. They get around in all sorts of ways—on wind, in water or even on a squirrel's bushy tail. Let's solve the mystery of how seeds travel.

Many travel on the wind. Their seed pods split open, and when the stems bend in the wind, the seeds are sent flying. When poppy seeds are ready, the top of the seed pod pops open. When the wind blows, the seeds come out tiny holes around the rim. They're like salt in a shaker!

Some seeds have little parachutes. When the wind blows, tiny hairs open and catch the breeze. These seeds, like the dandelion in this picture, can travel far. Others, like maple seeds, fly with wings and look like tiny propellers turning in the breeze.

Lots of seeds travel in water. They're carried by creeks and rivers or ocean currents. Hard-shelled coconuts float and can cross oceans, riding on the salt water.

A water lily grows in lakes and ponds. Its floating seeds have jelly coatings. Fish sometimes eat the seeds and carry them far. They can pass right through the fish and fall to the bottom of a stream, pond or lake and grow.

Many animals besides fish scatter seeds. Birds and squirrels often bury seeds. Some seeds have little barbs and stick to animal's fur or people's clothing. Have you ever walked through a field and gotten stickers in your socks? Those were seeds looking for a free ride!

DISAPPEARING SEEDS

Some plants scatter seeds all by themselves, like these impatiens. The seeds don't need to wait for rides on wind, water or animals. Instead, they shoot like tiny rockets out of seed pods, and seem to disappear.

Impatiens are pretty flowers for shady places. When a flower is pollinated, the seed pod in the center grows, getting bigger and bigger. Soon the petals fall off, and the pod stretches and grows as far as it can.

Bang! It pops! Seeds spray out everywhere. The force curls the sides of the pod like little ribbons. Have the seeds really disappeared? No. The seeds fly a few feet and fall to the ground.

Other plants have popping pods, too. Wood sorrel is a small plant that looks like clover with little yellow flowers. It makes a little seed pod with tiny slits in the side.

Inside, the seeds are coated with a slippery gel. When the seeds are ripe, the pod swells and gets very tight. Then, bang! The slick seeds shoot right out of the slits in the side. If you touch a ripe wood sorrel pod, you can watch this action.

Look closely at an impatiens flower to see the tiny green center. After pollination, the green ovary swells as new seeds form inside.

The pod swells and gets big. When touched, it will pop open. If it doesn't, it's not quite ready and will soon burst open on its own.

As the sides snap, seeds are thrown in all directions. Some of the seeds will land in places where they can sprout and grow.

CYCLES IN NATURE

Plants of all kinds produce seeds. We know the cycle goes from flower to seed and starts again. But the cycles aren't all the same. Some are over quickly; others go on and on. Let's find out why.

Plants that live and die in one year are called *annuals*. They sprout, grow flowers, make seeds and die in one year. Many flowers and most vegetables are annuals. In your test garden, sweet alyssum, cosmos, strawflowers, marigolds, sunflowers and tomatoes are annuals.

Other plants have a two-year cycle. They're called *biennials*. Biennials spend most of their energy the first year making roots and leaves. The next year they make flowers and seeds, then die. Foxgloves, pansies, English daisies and forget-me-nots are biennials.

Perennials have longer life cycles. They grow from seed and live longer than two years. Many perennials die to the ground in winter but grow back from their roots in the spring. Daylilies, yarrow and lavender are perennials.

Can you guess why plants have so many different cycles? The answer is survival. Some use all their energy in one year to make seeds for the next year. Others make many seeds over time. Each has developed the right cycle for its own needs.

Perennials Perennials, like these lavender plants, have a longer cycle. Their green tops remain or grow back from the roots year after year.

Annuals These marigolds are annuals. They grow, flower and make seeds in one year.

Biennials These English daisies are biennials. They grow for two years and then start over from seed.

SEEDS THAT GROW UNDERGROUND

Peanuts are not really nuts but seeds that come from the pea family. Peanuts are unusual because their seeds form underground. Let's figure out how peanuts hide their seeds.

After pollination, the flowers that make peanuts will fade and lose their petals.

The flower stalk, or peg, will curve and grow down into the soil. The peanuts form underground.

The leaves send food down to the peanut seeds growing under the ground.

THE PEANUT PLANT

The peanut has two kinds of bright yellow flowers. Only one kind can make seeds. The flowers that make seeds do something strange after they're pollinated. When the flower fades, the stalk, or *peg* curves down and grows into the soil. The peanuts form underground in a pod or shell.

Peanuts are easy and fun to grow. Start with raw—not roasted—peanuts. Grocery stores often sell them. Take a peanut from the shell and plant it about an inch deep in potting soil. Water it well. Keep it in a warm, sunny spot, and soon the round leaves and strong stalks will pop up.

After frosts are over, transplant the seedling to a warm part of the garden in full sun. The peanut likes loose, soft, sandy soil. Let it grow all summer and water it regularly. When the plant turns yellow, carefully loosen the soil around it and pull it up. Before you take the peanuts off, let the vines dry in a warm, dark place for two to three weeks. If you live in a cold climate with a short growing season, your plant may not have time to make many peanuts.

GROWING ALFALFA SPROUTS

Here's a vegetable you can grow in a couple of days. The seedlings won't need soil because sprouts get eaten before all the food stored in the seed is used up.

Sprouting Alfalfa Seeds

First Put about a tablespoon of alfalfa seeds in a jar with water. Let them soak overnight. Use more seeds if your jar is larger than this pint jar.

Third Wait three days for the seeds to sprout and grow. Put them in a bowl with water. Skim off the hulls, watching for hard unsprouted seeds.

Second Use a rubber band to fasten cheesecloth over the opening of the jar. Drain the water. Rinse sprouts twice a day. Leave jar tilted upside-down in a bowl in a dark spot.

Last Drain the sprouts. Put them in a clear container with air holes. After a day or two near a sunny window, the sprouts will turn green and be ready to eat.

MEASURING SEED PRODUCTION

IMPROVING THE ODDS

Tomatoes taste delicious when you grow your own. You can start them indoors four to five weeks before the warm weather comes. Or, if you have a long growing season, you can wait and plant them outside. If you don't have space in the garden, try growing a cherry tomato plant in a container.

Let's follow one tomato plant and see what happens. After your plant gets going, little yellow flowers will appear. When pollinated, the flowers will form tomatoes with seeds inside.

Keep track of how many tomatoes your plant makes and write this in a notebook. If you cut open a tomato, you'll see lots of seeds inside. How many do you think there are? Make a guess, and multiply that by the number of tomatoes you pick. You'll see that thousands of seeds are produced by just one plant.

Tomatoes and all flowering plants produce as many flowers and seeds as they can. The reason why is easy to see. You may already have the answer. Plants, like this tomato, produce lots and lots of seeds for survival. Not all of the seeds end up with the right conditions to grow. The more seeds a plant makes, the better chance seedlings have of sprouting and growing up.

Healthy plants are the ones with the right amount of water, air, food, light and space. Do healthy plants make more seeds? Yes. They grow more flowers and more seeds because they are strong. And, the seeds they make will be strong, too. That keeps the cycle going—giving us plenty of red, juicy tomatoes to enjoy.

TESTING SEED STRENGTH

Seeds work very hard to sprout. Let's do a test to see how strong they are. Here, scarlet runner bean seeds must grow through hardened plaster.

For the test you'll need seeds, a can and plaster from the hobby store. First soak a few scarlet runner bean seeds in water overnight.

Next spread newspapers over your work area. With an adult helper, mix plaster and water in the can, according to the directions on the box of plaster. The plaster should be smooth and thick, like whipping cream. Wait about fifteen minutes for it to begin to set.

Now push the seeds about 1/2 inch deep into the plaster. The seeds should be a few inches apart. Smooth the plaster over the seeds. Before long, it'll be hard as rock!

Choose a warm, sunny spot for the can. Pour a little water on the plaster each day. After a week or more you'll see cracks. Soon the seeds will push up and break the plaster. Did all of your seeds make it? Only the strongest can break through.

The little plants cannot get nutrients from the plaster. But the bean seeds have enough food stored to keep the seedlings alive for weeks. These seeds worked hard to sprout. How strong they are!

Strong seeds can break through plaster and send out roots. In nature they grow through hard soil.

Soaking the seeds in water overnight makes them swell so they can open and sprout.

The powdery plaster, when mixed with water, becomes hard as rock.

SEED SURVIVAL

Seeds are tough. This picture shows new plants growing from seeds that went through a fire. The seeds stayed alive even though the plants died. Then, when the time was right, they sprouted. Let's see what seeds can take and still grow.

WHAT ARE THEY WAITING FOR?

Fires, floods, freezes, chemicals, even years of waiting won't stop some seeds from growing. This helps the plant world to survive after all kinds of disasters.

Seeds can survive fires, like the one that swept through these hills. When the seeds sprout, the hills turn green again. Seeds survive floods and droughts and replace plants that are lost. Seeds can stand freezing cold. They live through frozen winters and begin to grow when the weather warms.

Some seeds need to go through rough conditions before they can sprout. There are seeds that need the high heat of a fire to break down their seed coats. The fire clears the area of plants that compete for water, air, light and nutrients. This gives the new seeds a better chance to make it.

Certain seeds survive a long time. Scientists once found 1000-year-old lotus seeds buried under a dry lake bed. Long ago the lotus plants made seeds as big and hard as marbles. These sank to the bottom of the lake.

When the scientists softened the hard seed coats, the seeds grew into beautiful lotus plants with big pink flowers. Today, if you scratch a lotus seed, it'll sprout in a few days.

There are chemicals in nature that help soften seed coats. The chemicals inside the stomachs of animals sometimes work. After the seed gets eaten and goes through the animal, it can grow.

Through all this rough and sometimes strange treatment, seeds stay alive. And, they never lose track of when it's time to grow.

SENSITIVE PLANTS

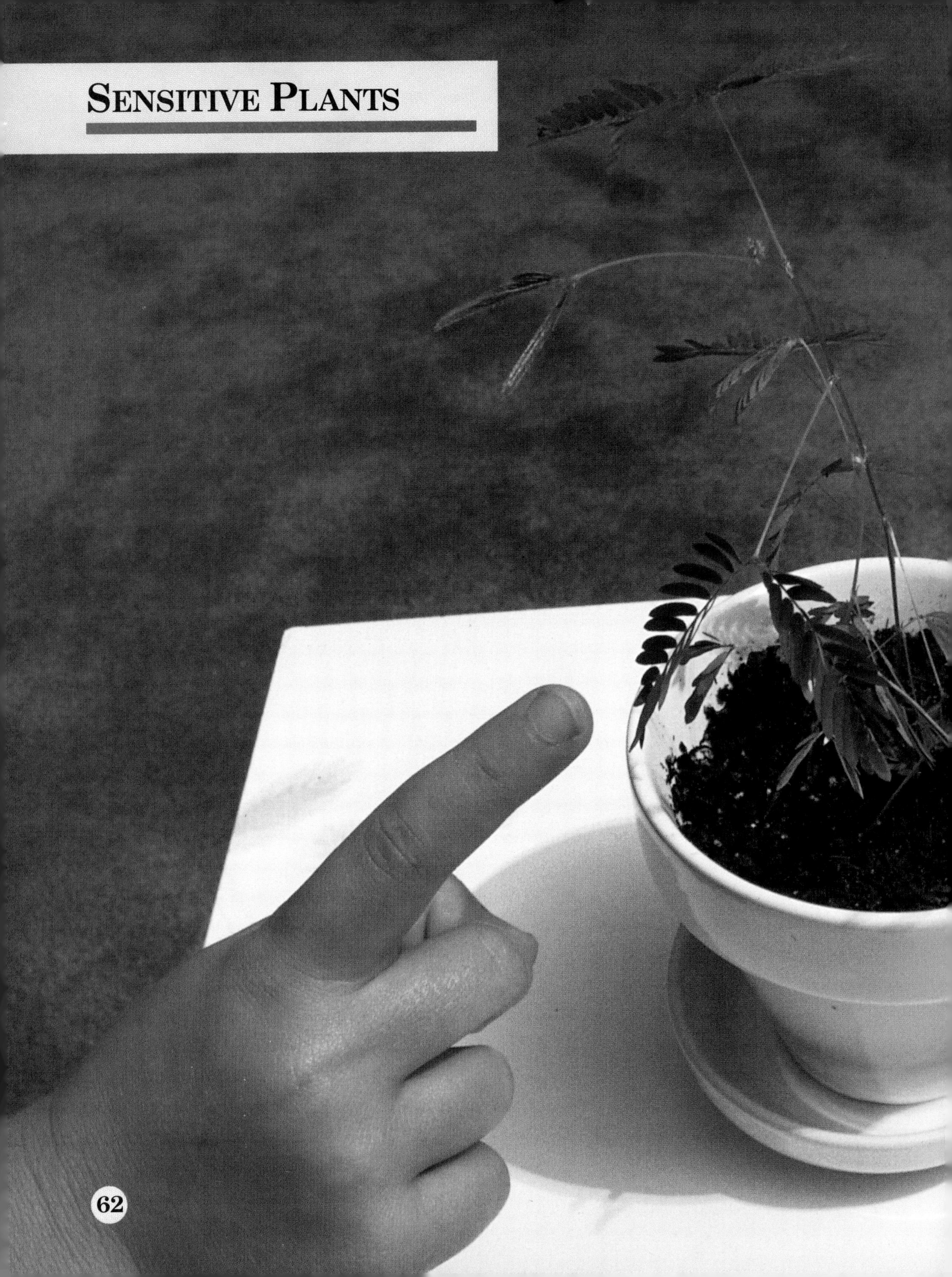

MOVING PARTS

Here's a very unusual house plant you can grow from seed. It's called a *sensitive plant*. An amazing thing happens when you touch its leaves. They move! When touched, the leaves close up. But after a few minutes they open again.

What makes a sensitive plant close up? Do other plants move like this? Let's see if we can solve these mysteries.

The sensitive plant has leaves that line up opposite each other like pages in a book. At night or when touched lightly, the leaves fold together like a book closing shut (see photo below). A stronger touch makes the stems droop. Scientists think the plants may do this to keep animals from eating its leaves.

Another plant with moving leaves is the venus flytrap. It has two opposite leaves that open up, also like pages in a book. On the edges of the leaves are tiny spikes like fingers. The inside of the leaves have a sticky surface. When an insect touches the sticky part it can get stuck. Then the leaf slowly closes together, and the critter trapped inside becomes food for the plant.

You can see plants have found some interesting ways to survive.

DRIED FLOWERS

Many flowers can be dried by hanging them upside down. Pick fresh, dry blooms that are not yet fully open. Remove the leaves, bunch three to six flowers with string, and hang them in a dark, dry place for two or three weeks.

Using Silica Gel

Pour about 1 inch of gel in the bottom of a flat container. Stick each flower into the gel, stem down. Make sure the flowers don't touch.

Carefully pour the gel around each flower, keeping the flower upright. Cover completely, taking care not to bend the petals. Close the container and seal the lid with tape. Check the flowers in one week.

OTHER WAYS TO DRY

Another way to dry flowers is with silica gel. Silica gel is made of dry particles that look like shiny white sand with bits of blue mixed in. The gel acts like a sponge, absorbing water from the flower.

You can buy silica gel in most hobby stores. It's easy to use. Here are some hints.

Use a flat container with a very tight lid, like a cookie tin. If you are drying more than one flower, make sure the flowers don't touch. That way the gel completely surrounds each flower.

Pick your flowers on a warm, sunny day when the petals are dry and the blooms not fully open. Leave an inch or two of stem.

You can dry all kinds of flowers in silica gel, including pansies, marigolds, roses, daisies, carnations and cosmos.

Remember that the flowers are fragile. When you check to see if they're dry, carefully brush away the gel. If the flower is ready, the petals will be crisp, like fine paper.

You can reuse the silica gel if you heat it in the oven. When the gel has taken in too much moisture, the blue crystals will turn pink. To reuse the gel, ask an adult helper to heat the gel in a shallow pan in a 300 degrees F. oven until the pink crystals turn blue again. Cool the gel and store it in an airtight container.

PRESSED FLOWERS

Pressing flowers is an easy way to save them. You can press the sweet alyssum from your test garden. Other flowers work, too. Thin flat ones are the easiest and dry the quickest. You can also press leaves and stems.

Dear Grandma,

I just wanted to let you know how much I enjoyed your visit. Thank you for the presents and for helping me in the garden.

Love,
Elizabeth

How to Press Flowers

Many flowers are easy to press, including cosmos, forget-me-not, geranium, pansy, Johnny-jump-up and phlox.

Second Place a 1 inch stack of newspapers on top of one book. Tape a piece of white paper or a smooth white paper towel to the newspaper. This keeps the newspaper ink from staining your flowers.

First Pick your flowers when they look their best and are completely dry. Pick some leaves and stems, too. You'll need 2 heavy books, newspaper and white paper or paper towels.

Last Set the pansies face down on the white paper. Press the centers flat. Make sure the flowers don't touch or have folded petals. Cover with another sheet of white paper and more newspaper. Put the other book on top. Check the pansies in two weeks.

A BEAN MAGIC TRICK

Here's a trick with some very pretty beans you can grow from seeds. They're called *purple pod beans*. The beans grow in the late spring and summer. The plants have dark pink flowers that turn into purple pods.

The magic happens when the beans are cooked. They're purple going into the pot, but they come out green. What happens to the purple, and where does the green come from? Can you guess what makes the beans change?

The answer is heat. When the water boils, the heat changes the colors you see in the bean pods. The purple color breaks down, and soon you see the green underneath that was hidden by the purple.

The green in the beans is chlorophyll. Chlorophyll also changes in the hot water, making the beans get darker after cooking.

To grow purple pod beans, plant them outside in rows when the cold weather is over. Seed packets will tell you the best time for your area.

Plant one or two seeds together every 3 inches. Leave 1 1/2 feet between rows so the beans have room to grow. Pick them before they get too big. When you bring them in to cook, you'll have a little magic show in your own kitchen.

69

DRIED GOURDS

One interesting plant you can grow from seed is a gourd. Gourds, which are large fruits with hard shells, are related to pumpkins and cucumbers. But gourds are not good to eat!

Like the birdhouse gourd, most gourds come from vines that grow all summer. The vines need heat to make their unusual fruits.

Gourds have tough skins. Some are very bumpy and covered with warts. Some have unusual colors or stripes. Others have strange shapes, and some have long necks that can be tied in knots as they grow.

Gourds have been used by people all over the earth for thousands of years. Some scientists believe gourds were one of the first plants grown by man.

Most often gourds were used for containers. Today they are still made into bowls, plates, cups, spoons, sponges or even musical instruments. Many gourds are used for decorations.

Pick a gourd and let it dry in a cool spot inside. It may take as long as one to two months to dry completely and become hollow inside. When you shake it, the seeds will rattle. If you paint it or draw a design on it, you'll have a pretty musical instrument.

Make this birdhouse gourd with an adult friend and watch the birds move in!

Making a Birdhouse

First After your gourd is dry and hollow inside, wash it with soap and warm water.

Third Cut a 1 inch round hole about 6 inches from the bottom of the gourd. This will be the door of the house.

Second Coat the outside of the gourd with shellac, wax or paint. Birds like colors that aren't too bright. Let the coating dry completely, and coat again.

Last Poke a small hole near the top of the gourd. Put string or wire through the hole and hang your birdhouse from a tree.

TASTY SEEDS

ROASTING SUNFLOWER SEEDS

Sunflowers are interesting plants to grow from seeds. You can watch them grow bigger and bigger until they are taller than you. Sunflowers have a secret that birds have known about for years—their seeds taste great!

You can harvest and roast the seeds to enjoy their crunchy, nutty flavor. Ask your adult helper to come along.

Harvest the sunflower seeds at the end of summer. The flower will fade and lose most of its petals when it's ready. Put the seed head over a bag or tray and rub your hand over the face of the flower. This loosens the seeds so you can shake them free. Set them in the sun or a warm place until they are dry. It may take several days.

Now they're ready for roasting, which makes the seeds crisp. Spread the seeds in a single layer in a shallow pan. Sprinkle them with salt if you like.

With your helper, bake them in a preheated oven set at 300 degrees F. for 10–15 minutes. Turn them once or twice while they roast. Larger seeds will take a little longer.

Let them cool. To eat them, pop the seed in your mouth and crack the shell with your teeth. Spit out the shell and eat the seed inside.

ROASTING PUMPKIN SEEDS

That big pumpkin you've been waiting to carve is almost ready. The weeks of watering and wondering when it would turn from green to orange are over.

But this time, when you carve your jack-o'-lantern for Halloween, don't throw away the seeds. Roasted in the oven, they make a tasty snack. With an adult helper, you can turn the seeds into a great treat.

First wash off the stringy pulp from the seeds with cold water. Pat them dry. Next spread the seeds in a single layer on a cookie sheet so they don't touch. Sprinkle them with salt if you like.

Heat the oven to 300 degrees F. Bake the pumpkin seeds for 20–30 minutes. Check them often and turn them over once for even roasting. Larger seeds may take longer. They'll look dry and light brown when they're ready.

Cool the seeds. To eat them, split the shells and eat the nut. Some people like to eat the whole thing—shell and all—as a nutty, crunchy treat.

WILDFLOWERS

If you scatter a handful of wildflower seeds on the soil, you'll get bright, beautiful flowers like the ones in this field. Then nature takes over, keeping the cycle going year after year.

EASY CARE GARDENING

For a garden filled with color, try planting wildflower seeds. Wildflowers and native plants (those that grow naturally in an area) are special because they can grow without any help. In nature they have no choice.

Over time, wildflowers and natives have learned to live with the climate and soil conditions in their area. This is called *adaptation*. Do you know which plants and trees are native to your area?

To plant a wildflower garden, start by choosing wildflowers that grow where you live. Seed companies often sell packets of wildflowers for different regions. You might want to try a special mix that will attract birds or butterflies.

When you open the package of mixed wildflower seeds, you'll find seeds of different sizes and shapes. Some will sprout right away, some will wait. The seeds will grow into all different sorts of plants when the time is right.

Find a sunny spot in the garden. Your seed package will tell you how much space you need. Clear away any weeds or grasses. Loosen the soil with a fork, then rake it smooth.

Scatter the wildflowers by hand, tossing them all through the bed, not in one spot. Water the seeds with a light spray, or rake them into the soil and cover them with a fine layer of light soil or planting mix. If rain doesn't come, water the seeds regularly until the plants get going.

In a couple of weeks, you should see the first sprouts. Watch through the seasons as different plants flower and form seeds for the next year.

WORLD WITHOUT SEEDS

In great forests long ago, horsetails, known as *Equisetum hymale*, grew 100 feet high and 3 feet wide. Today they live in marshy areas and grow 4 feet tall.

Long ago, even before dinosaurs lived, the world did not have flowering plants or trees. It looked much different from our world today.

There were giant ferns as tall as trees. Horsetails, like the ones in this picture, grew as big as telephone poles. There were mosses and mushrooms, too, but no flowers or trees.

The earth was steamy and hot then. In huge, green, swampy forests, giant dragonflies and animals that looked like mighty salamanders prowled.

As time went on things changed. Dinosaurs appeared and so did the first seeds. Seeds arrived over 150 million years ago. Conifers, trees that make cones, made the first seeds on the scales of their cones.

Slowly, over millions of years, flowering plants developed. The first were flowering trees like elms, oaks and magnolias. Later, garden flowers, vegetables and wildflowers grew. Because of seeds—those amazing little packages of life—these plants soon covered the earth.

Today flowering plants give us all— humans and animals—a world we can live in. They give us food and medicine, wood for houses and cotton for clothes. Almost everything around us comes, in one way or another, from seeds and flowering plants. Without them, we'd be lost.

INDEX

A

Acorn, Oak tree seed, 27
Adaptation, wildflower and
    native plant, 75
Adult helpers, gardening, 41
Air, needed for sprouting,
    15–16
Alfalfa, sprouting, 54–55
Animals
    help with pollination, 11
    seeds scattered by, 47
Annuals, plant, 50
Anther, flower, 12
Apples, seeds in, 8
Avocado, sprouting an, 18–19

B

Bachelor's button (*Centaurea
    cyanus*), 39
Bananas, seeds in, 8
Beans
    edible plants, 25
    purple pod, 68–69
Bees, help with pollination, 11
Biennials, plant, 50–51
Birdhouse gourd, 70–71
Birds
    help with pollination, 11
    seeds scattered by, 47
Broccoli, edible vegetable, 24
Bugs, protecting seedlings
    from, 37
Butterflies, help with
    pollination, 11

C

Carrot, edible vegetable, 25
Celery, edible vegetable, 24
Centaurea cyanus, 39
Chlorophyll
    bean magic trick and, 68–69
    used to make plant food, 23
Coconut
    how they travel, 47
    palm tree seed, 8, 27
Cone, Redwood tree seed, 27
Cosmos (*Cosmos* species)
    collecting seeds from, 44
    growing, 39
    growing dwarf, 31
    made of florets, 29
Cosmos species, 39
Cut flowers, growing, 38–39

D

Daisies, made of florets, 29
Dried flowers, 64–65
Dried gourds, 70–71
Dwarf cosmos, in test
    garden, 31

E

Easy care gardening, 75
Eatable plants, types of,
    24–25
Egg carton, to grow
    seedlings, 40
Egg carton planter,
    starting a, 33
Equipment, list of garden,
    40–41
Equisetum hymale, 76
Experiments
    bean magic trick, 68–69
    being a plant scientist, 43
    making a birdhouse gourd,
        70–71
    pollination, 42–43
    roasting sunflower and
        pumpkin seeds, 72–73
    with seedlings, 16–17
    seed lunch box, 17
    sprouting an avocado, 18–19
    test garden, 30–31
    testing seed strength,
        58–59

F

Female parts of flowers,
    listed, 11–12
Fertilizer, for seedlings, 37
Filaments, support flower
    anthers, 12
Florets, flowers which
    have, 29
Flowering plants, grown
    from seeds, 9
Flowers
    anther in, 12
    cut, 38–39
    dried, 64–65
    easy to grow, 38
    female and males parts of,
        11–12
    fragrant, 38–39
    how they make seeds, 10–11
    ovules, 12

petals, 12
pistils, 12
plant, 22–23
pollination in, 11, 42–43
pressed, 66–67
seeds in, 12
stalk or peg, 52–53
stamens in, 12
stem of, 12
sunflower, 28–29
Foods, which come from
    seeds, 6–7
Fork, garden, 40
Fragrant flowers, 38–39
Fruits
    plant, 23
    plant parts which are, 24–25

G

Gardening
    adult helpers with, 41
    caring for seedlings, 36–37
    easy care, 75
    equipment and tools for,
        40–41
    see also Planting
Gardens, seeds found in your,
    8–9
Geranium, floret clusters in, 29
Gourds, dried, 70–71

H

Hardening off, seedlings, 32
Help, adult, 41
Horsetails (*Equisetum
    hymale*), 76
House, seeds found in your,
    8–9

I

Iceland poppy, parts of, 12
Impatiens, seeds scattered
    by, 48–49

L

Leaves
    moving, 63
    plant, 22–23
    that trap insects, 63
Leggy seedlings, 32
Lettuce, 25

Life cycle
    nature, 50–51
    sweet pea seeds, 10–11
    of trees, 26–27
Light, needed for sprouting,
    15–16
Lobularia maritima, 38

M

Male parts of flowers, listed,
    11–12
Maple trees, seeds, 26
Marigold (*Tagetes* species)
    easy to grow, 38
    in test garden, 31
Markers, garden, 40
Mosses, 76
Mulch, seedlings need, 37
Mushrooms, 76

N

Native plants, adaptation of, 75
Nature life cycle, 50–51
Nutrients, needed for
    seedlings, 16–17

O

Oak tree, seeds, 27
Ovules, seeds-to-be, 12

P

Palm tree, seeds, 8, 26–27, 47
Peanuts
    life cycle of, 52–53
    seeds in, 9
    sprouting, 53
Peas, 24
Peg, peanut, 52–53
Perennials, plant, 50–51
Petals
    flower, 12
    sunflower, 28
Phlox drummondii, 39
Phlox (*Phlox drummondii*), 39
Pine cones, seeds in, 8
Pistil, flower, 12
Planting
    indoors, 32–33
    outdoors, 34–35
    see also Gardening
Plants
    annual, 50
    benefits of, 76

78

biennial, 50–51
eatable fruit, 24–25
eatable vegetable, 24–25
flowering, 9, 22–23
food factories in, 22–23
fruit of, 23
leaves, 22–23
native, 75
parts which are eaten,
    24–25
perennial, 50–51
roots, 22–23
sensitive, 62–63
stems, 23
Pods
    popping, 48–49
    seeds grown inside, 10–11
Pollen
    experiment with, 42–43
    made from male part of
        flower, 11–12
Pollination
    experiment, 42–43
    flower, 11
Poppy seeds, 7, 45
Pressed flowers, 66–67
Pumpkin, roasting seeds, 73
Purple pod beans, 68–69

R
Rake, garden, 40
Ray flowers, sunflower
    petals, 28
Redwood trees, seeds, 26
Roots, plant, 22–23

S
Secret code, inside seeds, 9
Seedlings
    bug protection for, 37
    experiment with, 16–17
    fertilizer for, 37
    garden care for, 36–37
    grow into plants, 10
    hardening off, 32
    leggy, 32
    mulching for, 37
    snail and slug protection
        for, 37
    started indoors, 32–33
    started outdoors, 34–35
    thinning, 35
    transplanting, 35

Seed lunch box experi-
    ment, 17
Seed packets, reading
    information on, 38, 41
Seeds
    built-in time clocks in, 21
    coconut, 8, 26–27, 47
    collecting or harvesting,
        44–45
    defining, 9
    eating tasty, 72–73
    egg carton planter for,
        33, 40
    evolution of, 76
    flower, 9–12
    foods which come from,
        6–7
    found in foods, 8–9
    found in house or garden,
        8–9
    grown in water, 18
    how they travel, 46–47
    kernels of corn, 9
    life cycle of, 10–11
    measuring production of, 56
    natural chemicals soften
        coats of, 61
    parachutes of, 47
    in peanuts, 9
    planting indoors, 32–33
    planting outdoors, 34–35
    pollination of, 11
    scattering wildflower,
        74–75
    secret code for growing, 9
    secret plant information
        in, 27
    sprouting, 14–15
    surviving disasters, 60–61
    testing strength of, 58–59
    tree, 26–27
    underground, 52–53
    see also Planting;
        Sprouting
Sensitive plants, 62–63
Silica gel, drying flowers
    with, 65
Slugs, protecting seedlings
    from, 37
Snails, protecting seedlings
    from, 37
Soil
    needed for sprouting, 15–16

Sprouting
    an avocado, 18–19
    built-in time clocks for, 21
    a peanut, 53
    seeds, 14–15
    seed strength for, 58–59
    see also Planting; Seeds
Sprouts, growing alfalfa,
    54–55
Stakes, garden, 40
Stalk, flower, 52–53
Stamens, flower, 12
Stems
    flower, 12
    plant, 23
Strawberries, seeds in, 9
Strawflower, in test garden, 31
String, garden, 40
Sunflower
    florets in, 29
    ray flowers in, 28
    roasting seeds, 72
    seeds in center of, 28
    in test garden, 30
Sweet alyssum (*Lobularia
    maritima*)
    easy to grow, 38
    in test garden, 31
Sweet peas, pod seeds, 10–11

T
Tagetes species, 38
Test garden, growing a, 30–31
Thinning seedlings, 35
Tomatoes
    growing, 57
    seeds in, 8
    in test garden, 30
Tools, garden, 40–41
Transplanting seedlings, 35
Trees, life cycle of, 26–27
Trowel, garden, 40

U
Underground seeds, 52–53

V
Vegetables
    growing alfalfa sprouts,
        54–55
    plant parts which are, 24–25
Venus flytrap, 63
Verbena hybrida, 39

W
Water
    big seeds grown in, 18
    needed for sprouting, 15–16
    seeds travel on, 47
    soaking seeds in, 58
Watering, garden seedlings,
    36–37
Water lily, 47
Weeding, garden, 37
Wildflower seeds, 74–75
Wind, seeds travel on the, 47
Wood sorrel, 48

Z
Zinnia elegans, 38
Zinnia (*Zinnia elegans*), 38

A NOTE FROM NK LAWN AND GARDEN CO.

For more than 100 years, since its founding in Minneapolis, Minnesota, NK Lawn and Garden has provided gardeners with the finest quality seed and other garden products.

We doubt that our leaders, Jesse E. Northrup and Preston King, would recognize their seed company today, but gardeners everywhere in the U.S. still rely on NK Lawn and Garden's knowledge and experience at planting time.

We are pleased to be able to share this practical experience with you through this ongoing series of easy-to-use gardening books.

Here you'll find hundreds of years of gardening experience distilled into easy-to-understand text and step-by-step pictures. Every popular gardening subject is included.

As you use the information in these books, we hope you'll also try our lawn and garden products. They're available at your local garden retailer.

There's nothing more satisfying than a successful, beautiful garden. There's something special about the color of blooming flowers and the flavor of home-grown garden vegetables.

We understand how special gardening is to you—it's important to NK Lawn and Garden, too. After all, we've been a friend to gardeners everywhere since 1884.